The Ghost of
Able Mabel

GHOSTLY TALES

Look out for more stories...

The Spectre of Hairy Hector

The Ghost of
Able Mabel

Penny Dolan
illustrated by Philip Hopman

To Jim, Tom and Eleanor,
with love and thanks

This edition produced for the Book People Ltd,
Hall Wood Avenue, Haydock, St Helens WA11 9UL

First published by Scholastic Ltd, 1997
This edition published by Scholastic Ltd, 2005

Text copyright © Penny Dolan, 1997
Illustrations copyright © Philip Hopman, 1997
Cover illustration copyright © Klaas Verplancke, 2003

ISBN 0 439 95485 1

Printed and bound by Nørhaven Paperback A/S, Denmark

The right of Penny Dolan and Philip Hopman to be identified as the author
and illustrator of this work respectively has been asserted by them in accordance
with the Copyright, Designs and Patents Act, 1988.

Chapter One

Over a hundred years ago, young Sam
Sprockett lived with his grandfather in a
small stone cottage. Outside the cottage ran
a path, but nobody ever, ever passed along
it. Sam wondered about that path. Below
him, the wide, worn stones of the path
wound down into Hopethwaite Village.
Above him, the path disappeared into the
looming darkness of Hagworth Fell. At night,
the grey moor-mist swirled down the becks
towards Sam's home.

The thin, black cat sat on Sam's sill and stared out at the moon with her bright blue eyes.

Hopethwaite folk were so poor they begged crumbs from the church mice on Sundays. Day by day, they went quietly about their business. Only the broad, bold cobbles of the village street told that Hopethwaite had once bustled with life.

One night, as Sam watched the kettle sing on the hearth, a question came into his head. He stroked and stroked the thin, black cat, but the question would wait no more.

"Grandad, why does no one use the path outside?"

Old Nathaniel sighed, and sucked at the stem of his clay pipe. "Lad, a terrible tale it is, but you shall hear it." The old man paused, gathering his thoughts. In the firelight, Sam saw to his astonishment that his grandfather's face was bright with remembered happiness.

"Once, Sam," Nathaniel began, "Hopethwaite was full of pretty shops and the rowdy calls of the great market..."

Sam nearly fell off his seat. "Here? If a sheep runs along Hopethwaite street, people talk about it for days! You say there was a market?"

"Aye, the grandest market hereabouts, stretching from top to bottom of the village! I'd long to go to Hopethwaite to see the sights."

Sam's eyes were wide as potlids. "Didn't you live in this cottage then, Grandad?"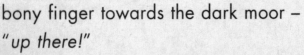

"Nay! When I was but fourteen, I lived –" Nathaniel pointed a bony finger towards the dark moor – "*up there!*"

"On the Hagworth Fell?" cried Sam. "*You?* You told *me* I must never go up there!"

"Sam, 'twas different days. That very path outside was the one roadway for all comers. Folk would be always passing on it, carrying their goods – cloth and cheese, flour and fish, salt and spices, gewgaws and nick-nacks and all manner of finery."

"But weren't folk afeared? Isn't the moor a big, broad step to cross, Grandad?"

"Right, Sam, but then nobody minded that it took more than a day from t'other side to this. Midway across was the haven of the Halfway Inn. Outside it might be wind and mire, but inside, on the welcoming hob, bubbled brimming stew-pots. Sam, that was where I was living, happy as the hours were long, serving the folk travelling to and from Hopethwaite Market."

Old Nathaniel sighed wistfully, and puffed at his pipe. He patted Sam's shoulder.

"It wasn't only I who lived there. The inn belonged to young Widow Warmley, barely more than a lass herself. Comfort by name and comfort by nature. She was as cheerful as a cherry pie – until that dark night..."

Chapter Two

Sam saw a tear burst from the old man's eye. "What happened?" he asked.

The old man gave a deep sob and began. "Oh, it was on a dark and stormy night..."

"Aye, Grandad," said Sam, stroking the thin, black cat. "It would be."

"Come eight o'clock and dinner just served, the front door of the inn crashed open, and a huge figure stood there, with the howling wind tossing her thatch of wiry hair about.

On her shoulder crouched an evil-looking, grey macaw with a yellow eye. Comfort Warmley's mouth dropped open.

"'Mabel?' she gasped. 'Is that you?'

"The woman gave a wicked grin. Her gold teeth glinted ominously in the candlelight.

"Broad she was as a bolster, but there was no comfort in her look. A coarse apron, spotted with stains from every sea-port in the world, wrapped her round. As she strutted her way between the tables, her boot-heels hit like hammers on the boards.

"Mabel reached the bar, and lolling back, took a large cigar from behind her ear. She puffed foul-smelling smoke into plump rings that floated upwards against the ceiling. Glasses stayed half-raised to lips, soup-spoons stayed unsupped, and not a word was spoken. The puddings sat trembling in their dishes.

"Comfort Warmley grasped a stripy tea-towel desperately to her bosom. 'Sister? What is it you want?'

"Mabel cackled. 'Surely you hadn't forgotten, Comfort? How I told you I'd return from the Seven Seas one day?'

"She took six large pickled onions from the jar on the counter, and swallowed five down. The last she held out teasingly between her fingers. The grey parrot hopped up and down greedily on her shoulder.

"'Stay, Barnacle! Stay!' Mabel commanded, as she walked around the room again. ''Tis a pleasant place you have, our Comfort,' Mabel said. 'I'll enjoy myself here.'

"'You're stopping?' said Comfort, turning pale.

"Mabel laughed. 'You wouldn't turn away your long-lost sister? What have we here?' Mabel sniffed at the saucepans of rich stew. 'Ttch! Tch! You're spoiling your guests, I see...'

"Mabel tossed the onion up in the air.

"The waiting macaw caught it and crunched it down.

"'Yes, spoiling these lily-livered land-lubbers! Always were too soft-hearted, Comfort. I'm the one that knows how to treat 'em.' Mabel's gaze slid like grease across the bar-room tables until she spotted old Bill Snoraway.

"'What do I see here?' Mabel bellowed furiously, pointing at Bill's plate."

"What was it, Grandad?" gasped Sam.

Nathaniel Sprockett shook his head. "A corner of burnt pie-crust. Poor Bill had hardly a tooth in his head to chew with.

He'd only stopped sucking at the piecrust out of politeness.

"Mabel's eyes narrowed. 'You lily-livered layabout! You wastrel of a worm!' she roared at poor Bill. 'Not one man on the bad ship *Tarantula* would dare to leave a single crumb...'

"'Don't, Mabel,' said Comfort. 'Bill can't help it. He gives me a good tip...'

"'A good tip? I'll give him a good tip!' Mabel cried, grabbing old Bill by the ankles and turning him upside down.

"She shook him until a handful of money
rattled down on to the floor, and then she
let go. She grabbed up the coins, and
stowed them briskly into her pocket.

"Then she gazed sternly around the inn. Suddenly everyone was eating away as if their life depended on it.

"Bill lay groaning on the floor. Every piece of crust or bone or gristle was vanishing from the plates. Even a stray beetle that had paused for a second on a saucer met a sudden end down someone's throat.

"'That's better!' Mabel said. 'Now, you idle layabout...' ("That was me, Sam," Nathaniel explained) '...show me the very best room. And bring me a dish of buttered muffins and a pint of best grog.'

"'I say!' The traveller from the very best room stood up to protest.

"Mabel looked at him sharply, and began rolling up her sleeves. 'Your things will be in the corridor, sir – or do you prefer them tossed into the horse-trough? I could even help you join them!'

"The traveller sat down again quickly. Suddenly, Mabel snatched the little leather menu-book that hung from Comfort's belt.

"'So what slops have you been serving them? Breakfast: Creamy porridge. Bacon and eggs.' Mabel extracted a pencil stub from her thick thatch of hair, and scribbled furiously over the pages.

"'That's better. Gruel, dry bread and giblets – that'll be good enough for them... What's this? Afternoon tea? Scones with strawberry jam? Shiver me timbers! Ships' biscuits from now on – with a good wobbling of weevils! And my very own mystery mince for dinner!'

"Someone gasped. Mabel snatched a plate from a table and lobbed it across the room. There was a cry of pain. Mabel's parrot danced up and down with laughter.

"'Don't you lot dare complain!' she snarled. 'You make good money from crossing the moor, with all your selling and dealing. Now the Halfway Inn will make good money too! I'm in charge now – me, Able Sea-Cook Mabel Spight – known throughout the Seven Seas as Able Mabel! I'll teach my sweet sister Comfort how an inn should be run, so I will.'

"Mabel pointed to a vast pile of sea-trunks. 'Move them up sharpish, lad!' she told me, stomping upstairs to her new room.

"'Who's a pretty girl then?' shrieked Barnacle the parrot.

"'I am,' cackled Able Mabel. 'I am!'"

Chapter Three

Old Nathaniel drew out a large spotted handkerchief and blew his nose loudly.

"Grandad?" said Sam. "Are you all right?"

Nathaniel shuddered. Sam handed him a cup of tea with three spoons of sugar.

Then he put down a saucer of milk for the thin, black cat, and asked, "What happened then?"

"Lad! The terrible times had begun. Folk who crossed Hagworth Fell still had to use the Halfway Inn, but all the welcome had gone. That woman had her portrait painted and hung it outside –

the sign of The Able Mabel. It was bad enough having her grim face outside, but to meet her inside the inn was even worse. Never a moment's kindness to anyone. All she wanted was money."

Sam tried to soothe the old man with some hot, buttered toast, but his grandad looked at him with wild eyes.

"When guests wanted food, what were
they served, Sam? Scum-soup, maggot-
muffins and mouse-pie. When they wanted
a fire, she set one thin twig blazing in the
hearth. When they wanted a good night's
sleep, there was naught but bare boards
and bedbug blankets. Even when they
tried to cheer themselves with chat, all
they got were Mabel's tales of terror on
the Seven Seas."

"Surely nobody paid good money for that?" said Sam.

His grandfather shrugged. "They had no choice, Sam. Remember, that path is the only way across Hagworth Fell! A gang of footpads began attacking lonesome travellers. Even Able Mabel's inn seemed safer than meeting those robbers. Of course, other folk only had to stay at the inn for one night..." his voice dropped to a whisper...

"but I – I still lived on like a poor slavey."

"Oh, Grandad!" said Sam. "What about Mistress Comfort Warmley?"

Sam's grandfather shook his head. "Ah, sadness indeed. When barely a week had gone by, Comfort did not come downstairs one morning. Mabel said Comfort was resting with a headache. The next day a notice was nailed to Comfort's door.

Do Not Disturb.
or Else.

"Of course I knew at once it was Mabel's writing! I scribbled a note, planning our escape, and pushed it secretly under Comfort's door. I heard a faint scuffling noise inside. That evening, Mabel eyed me coldly.

The next day I took along another note, but
Comfort Warmley's door was ajar and her
room was empty!"

"What happened?" asked Sam.

Nathaniel blew his nose on a large, red spotted handkerchief. "I never knew."

The thin, black cat wound around their ankles, miaowing at them. Sam scratched behind her pointed ears. She purred thankfully, and blinked her blue eyes.

"In the end," said Nathaniel, "folk would rather be blasted by the blizzards than shelter in her inn. The travellers went off to find other markets, and the Hopethwaite streets became as they now are – empty and silent."

"At least you didn't have so much work to do?" Sam suggested brightly.

His grandfather groaned. "Lad, I had twice as much! Mabel's gang of footpads moved in. They were the crew of the bad ship *Tarantula*, of course. They spent their time carousing, quarrelling and sleeping.

The jokes were even worse than the snores, and their habits were too awful to speak of." The old man shuddered.

"Grandad, why didn't *you* just leave?" said Sam.

"Sam, all the wealth I had in the world was there, in that inn. Each week, Comfort Warmley had paid one gold coin into the wooden box on the kitchen table.

It was my wage. I had food and lodging enough at the inn, and small coins from the customers if I needed cash to spend. So seven years'-worth of good gold lay in that box. How else was I to live? I had wanted a good start to my life!"

The old man looked around the small cottage, and the pieces of paltry furniture. On the mantelpiece were faded pictures of his family, now all dead and gone.

All he had left was young Sam. Nathaniel
gazed fondly at the boy.

"One evening, Sam, I sneaked up to
that wee box on the table, but the brass key
had gone from the lock! I found it
soon enough – hanging around the neck
of Mabel's macaw. I asked Mabel for
my money, but she only grinned horribly.
Tomorrow, Nathaniel, she would say, ask
me tomorrow..."

"She's nothing but a rotten stinking thief, that mean old Mabel!" burst out Sam. "If it was my money..."

"Now then, lad, that's easy to say. I waited on, and on, and time and again I tried to get that key, but it was no use." He held out his hand, and Sam saw faint beak-shaped scars on the skin. "At last, I gave up. I came down here to Hopethwaite, and lived as best I could."

"Without the money?"

"Aye. The box is still at the inn."

"Grandad, that was ages and ages ago. Why didn't you go back and get the box?" said Sam, waving his fist in the air.

"Lad, you must have heard the stories. They say 'tis only a fool would set foot in that inn."

"Surely that old Mabel Spight can't be there now?"

Outside an owl hooted in the night.

Nathaniel shivered and poked the fire up.

When it was burning brightly again, and the shadows had gone, he continued.

"Ah, Sam! Mabel and her mob fell out soon enough. Folk heard their clashing cutlasses and curses down in Hopethwaite. Mabel, so they say, gave a terrible, deadly scream that lasted a whole ten minutes. Then an awful quiet descended on the moor. The next dawn saw the whole ruffianly gang sailing out from Seaholt harbour – without their Able Sea-Cook."

"Grandad, tell me!" insisted Sam. *"What about Mabel?"*

Old Nathaniel took hold of his walking stick, and scratched five letters in the ashes on the hearth.

GHOST

The candle guttered as a sudden chill filled the room.

"*Folks say that Mabel still haunts the Halfway Inn!* Where do you think the terrible moor-mist comes from? There were never such night-fogs around Hopethwaite when I was young. It is the stench from Mabel's ghastly brews, and she sends them down as a curse on the village..."

"And *your* wages are *still* on *her* table, Grandad!" said Sam angrily.

"Sam, Sam! Hush! Don't talk so loud. It's time for bed. Be grateful we at least have a roof over our head and a pillow under it."

The thin, black cat curled up cosily on Sam's warm blanket, but she did not purr.

Chapter Four

All night through, Sam tossed and turned. It wasn't fair! His grandfather had worked so long and lost so much! All his life, old Nathaniel had scrimped and starved and all the time his own money was no more than a day's walk away.

The thin, black cat crept up on to Sam's chest, as if she was trying to comfort him. Sam gazed into her blue eyes, hoping for an answer.

Early the next morning, Sam pulled on his clothes, tied on his tackety boots and crept out the door. This time he did not turn down the path towards the village. Instead, he climbed into the grey mist, searching for the stones that marked the way ahead. The path rose steeply, up and up. At the top, the mist rolled away long enough to show the wide emptiness of Hagworth Fell. Across the heather, far off, stood the grey skeleton of the deserted inn. Beside the path clustered dark reedy pools, ready to drag at any false step. Sam felt something brush softly against his leg. The thin, black cat had followed him.

"Go home, cat," said Sam.

"Miaow!" said the cat firmly, and padded forward ahead of him across the misty moor, with her tail tall in the air.

Sam was glad of the company. It was a long, long journey to the deserted building. The faded sign hung sullenly above the door, and grime covered the window-panes. Sam and the cat stood on the doorstep. White moths fluttered in the grey dusk.

"Miaow!" said the cat purposefully.

Sam lifted the latch, pushed, and the door creaked open. The room was scattered with broken furniture and cracked plates. Mouldering food festered where it had landed. Cobwebs hung from filthy glasses. There was no movement anywhere, and the air smelt heavy and stale. Only two things had no dust upon them – the kitchen table, and on it, the small wooden box. Next to the table hung a domed shape, draped in a filthy, fringed cloth.

"Miaow!" the cat warned Sam.

Sam nodded and tiptoed over. The box still had a tiny brass keyhole – and no key.

Very carefully, Sam turned to
the domed shape, and slid
the filthy shawl down to
the floor, uncovering an
ancient birdcage. Inside,
in the gloom, perched a
bedraggled, feathery
creature. A chain was

just visible around its neck. On the chain
hung the small brass key, glinting.

"Mabel's macaw!" gasped Sam.

The macaw made no move at all. Just a
sad, stuffed remnant of Mabel's reign, Sam
decided. Very gingerly, he opened out the
thin wire gate, and put his hand inside the
cage. He edged it towards the dim shape
of the bird, towards the key. Dust seemed
to shower from the grey feathers as
Sam stretched for the chain.
The catch undid easily,
and the key slithered
down into his palm.

"Caw!!"
screeched
the creature,
suddenly coming
to life. Its eyes
were bright as
brass and its

beak snapped like sharpened scissors.

"Ouch!" yelled Sam.

He pulled his hand back sharply from the
pecking spectre. The key fell, rattling down
into the filth on the floor of the cage.
The ghostly parrot hopped furiously and

fiercely on its perch. It gave a long, unearthly screech. Then it shut its blazing eyes and stayed still. Sam knew that Barnacle was daring him to put his hand in once again.

"Bother!" sighed Sam. "What now?"

"Miaow?" said the cat.

"All right." Sam sighed. "You have a go."

The thin, black cat jumped up on the table, and sidled over to the cage. She reached out a soft paw and tapped. The cage swung slightly. The parrot's eyelids flickered. The cat purred, and tapped the cage again. This time it swung more violently. The parrot opened two startled eyes. It opened its vicious beak and stuck out a wrinkled grey tongue.

"Caaaaaw!" the mouldering macaw screeched. "Mabel! Mabel! Mabel! Caaaw! Where's my pretty girl then?"

The thin, black cat sat back, put her head to one side, and licked a hind leg thoughtfully. Then suddenly, the little cat whopped the cage an almighty blow.

The parrot called out furiously, flustering and beating its ghostly wings as it rushed to get out of the rapidly rocking cage.

"Caaaaaaaw!" it cursed angrily, and like a frenzied mop, shot out after the thin, black cat. She slipped like smoke from the table, across the floor, and was out of the open door already. The parrot sped off after the cat, its ghastly eyes glowing with rage.

Sam smiled, reached into the empty cage, and lifted out the key. He slid it into the brass lock, turned it, and opened the box.

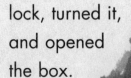

There, inside, lay a scattering of gold coins and a plump leather purse.

Two letters were on the purse: N.S. Nathaniel Sprockett. Sam thought how pleased his grandad would be.

Chapter Five

"OOOOoooOOOOH! BOY ABOARD!
OOOOOoooooooOOOOOH!"

A terrible sound echoed out of the gloom.
Shivers fell like water down Sam's spine. The
voice howled again. The glasses clinked and
shook on the shelves. There, in the half-light,
was forming a huge figure, draped in a
greasy apron. Her eyes glittered strangely,
and she rolled her ghostly sleeves up her
grisly arms. She looked very strong.

"STOP!" the figure cried, in a dreadful
voice.

"I AM THE GHOST OF MABEL SPIGHT! HOW DARE YOU COME TO MY INN TONIGHT?"

Holey-poley creepus! It's Able Mabel herself! thought Sam, turning to run. Then he remembered his poor grandfather. Sam spoke out, even though he was shaking with fright.

**"SHANT!
I MAY BE THE LAD
OF THE SHIVERING SOCKS,
BUT I'M TAKING THE MONEY
FROM THIS BOX!"**

Able Mabel's ghastly red eyes opened wider in surprise. She glided towards him.

Sam slid his fingers slowly towards his grandfather's bag of money.

"**STOP!**" the ghost declared.

"**I AM THE GHOST
OF HAGWORTH FELL
AND I'LL SMOTHER YOU UP
IN MY TERRIBLE SMELL!**"

Sam felt his stomach heave and tremble.
A stench of stale stew and mystery mince
flooded around him, into his hair and eyes
and nostrils, warm and wet and clammy.
It grew worse and worse with each moment.
Sam felt he would die unless he breathed
some good fresh air. Then Sam remembered
how Mabel had treated his grandfather, and
he spoke out, even though he was shivering
with fright.

**"TOUGH!
I MAY BE THE LAD
WITH THE TREMBLING TUMMY
BUT I'M HERE TO TAKE
MY GRANDAD'S MONEY!"**

Mabel's face turned a ghostly, ghastly green. Her smile glittered with dangerous gold.

"Miaow!" Sam heard the thin, black cat warn.

Just as Sam reached into the box for the money, Mabel gave a loud screech and the box slammed shut with all the money inside. He only just got his fingers out in time. Mabel's voice echoed around the room.

"BEWARE!" she howled,
**"I AM THE GHOST
OF ABLE MABEL
AND I SAY THE MONEY
STAYS ON THE TABLE!"**

Sam stared hard at the horrid, shadowy figure. He was very angry. Why shouldn't he take the wages down to his grandfather? What use did this old bully of a ghost have for it anyway? Sam snatched up the whole box, thrust it furiously into the safety of his jacket, and ran.

He yelled back, as loud as he could,

**"SO WHAT, OLD GHOSTLY-GUTS?
I AM THE GRANDSON
OF OLD NAT SPROCKETT
AND I SAY THE MONEY
STAYS IN MY POCKET!"**

Sam charged out of the inn door, off into the mist, searching for the path as he ran.

Behind came the sound of flapping feathers and rustling skirts, and a smell of parrot-cage and putrid food. Slowly, as Sam scurried through the night, the smell grew closer and closer, and the mist around grew thicker and thicker. He could hardly see the path.

"Cat! Come here!" Sam called anxiously as he ran. Where had the thin, black cat gone? She would get lost on the moor. "Cat!" he called, but his words echoed away through the mist.

Just as he reached the edge of Hagworth
Fell, Sam's tackety boots met the slippery
stones, and his feet shot from under him. He
toppled and fell, rolling and bouncing down
through the heather. Then he hit a rock and
lay still. He felt the money safe inside his
jacket, but he could hear Mabel's ghostly
skirts rustling towards him. Sam smelt

something like old, wet seaweed and
something moving up close to his cheek.

"Help! Get away!" he yelled.

**"I AM THE GHOST OF ABLE
MABEL..."** came the hollow voice as the
shape loomed over him.

Something like a small black shadow ran past Sam, and leaped up into the air. It was the thin, black cat, jumping and spitting, scratching and biting. The fearful figure recoiled from the cat's attack, and at that moment, the morning light burst through the mist.

Sam saw the cloud of fog churning and turning, as if Mabel was trying to wrap herself and the parrot away into the gloom.

Then, with an ear-splitting cry, the phantoms fluttered weakly and faded away.

Chapter Six

Sam raised his head, still panting, and
stared around at the purple heather.
The moor-mist grew paler. Soon it was
nothing but a white veil against the blue
morning sky. Sam stood up carefully.
Around, on the ground, lay a scattering
of grey feathers and a few strands of
smouldering seaweed.

"Sam! Sam, lad!" Up the steep fell-path
hobbled old Nathaniel. His face was

twisted with worry. "What have you been doing?"

Sam held out the box to his grandfather. "I've got it! I got your money back from Able Mabel!"

His grandfather glanced at the box, but it was his grandson he grabbed and hugged. "You're safe, my precious lad!" he cried. "Thank heaven!"

"Where's the black cat?" Sam said, twisting round. "Where's she gone?"

There was no sign of the thin, black cat, although they searched all that day for her.

Come evening, Sam and his grandfather sat by the fire. The box of money was hidden safely away.

Already folk had come up the path to hear Sam's tale. There was talk of treading the moor-path once again, and of setting the market stalls up in the street, and hurrahs and happiness such as Hopethwaite had not heard for years.

Then, just on midnight, there was a knock at the door. Sam went to open it. On the step stood an old lady wrapped in a black, woollen shawl. She smiled, and her cheeks dimpled like rose petals.

"Hello, young Sam," she said. "Can I
come in?" Sam nodded, puzzled. The old
woman went towards the fireplace.

"Nathaniel Sprockett?" she beamed.

Sam's grandfather looked up. His jaw dropped. His cheeks went bright red. His ears wiggled. "I don't believe it!" he said. "'Tis Comfort Warmley!"

"Aye, Nat. 'Tis I. After all this time," said the old lady. "Won't you ask me to sit down?"

Grandad Sprockett plumped up the cushions on the old armchair as if it was the queen of the world herself visiting their cottage. Comfort Warmley laughed and settled herself down, just as if she had always lived there. Sam brought her a cup of tea, and she supped it down cheerily.

"Aaah! 'Tis a long time since I tasted tea as good as that!" Comfort smiled across at Sam.

Sam saw, with astonishment, that her eyes were bright blue. Exactly the same blue as the eyes of the thin, black cat.

"You're a brave lad, Sam Sprockett," she said. "Good luck to you! Good luck to you indeed."

His grandad nodded happily.

GHOSTLY TALES

Prepare to shiver – the ghosts are here!
The strangest, scariest, *spookiest* spirits – back
from the past to haunt your bookshelf!

Look out for the next book in this shivery series!

The Spectre of Hairy Hector

Hairy Hector is just like his name. He's a grubby,
hairy, bad-tempered spectre – and he's living
in Jack and Aunt Arcady's new house!
Who was Hairy Hector, and why is he so cross?
The house is hiding deep, dark secrets.
Jack needs to search them out, but he doesn't
have much time...

Young Hippo
**Terrific stories, brilliant characters
and fantastic pictures – try one today!**

There are loads of fun books to choose from:

Jan Dean
The Horror of the Black Light

Alan MacDonald
The Great Brain Robbery

Penny Dolan
The Ghost of Able Mabel
The Spectre of Hairy Hector

Mary Hooper
Mischief and Mayhem!
Spooks and Scares!

Frank Rodgers
Head for Trouble!
Haunted Treasure!